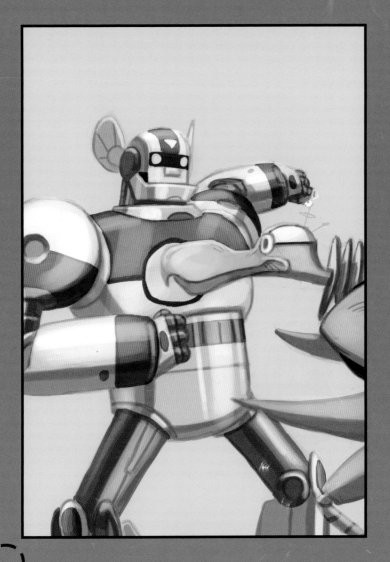

THE VOODOO VULTURES ATTACKED.

RIGHT
THUMB
HERE

THE VOODOO
VULTURES ATTACKED.

FLIP-O-RAMA 2

(pages 99 and 101)

Remember, flip *only* page 99.
While you are flipping, be sure you
can see the picture on page 99
and the one on page 101.
If you flip quickly, the two
pictures will start to look like
<u>one</u> *animated* picture.

Don't forget to add
your own sound-effects!

LEFT HAND HERE

RICKY'S ROBOT
FOUGHT BACK.

RIGHT
THUMB
HERE

RICKY'S ROBOT
FOUGHT BACK.

FLIP-O-RAMA 3

(pages 103 and 105)

Remember, flip *only* page 103.
While you are flipping, be sure you
can see the picture on page 103
and the one on page 105.
If you flip quickly, the two
pictures will start to look like
<u>one</u> *animated* picture.

Don't forget to add
your own sound-effects!

LEFT HAND HERE

THE VOODOO VULTURES
BATTLED HARD.

RIGHT
THUMB
HERE

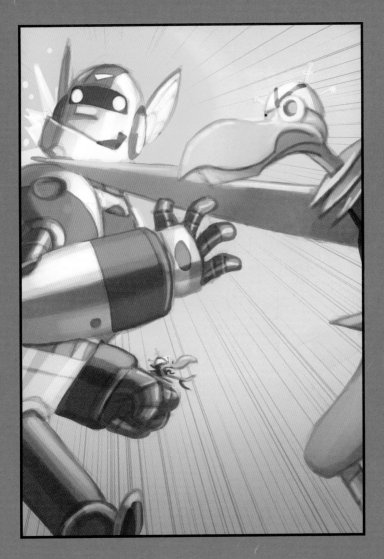

THE VOODOO VULTURES
BATTLED HARD.

FLIP-O-RAMA 4

(pages 107 and 109)

Remember, flip *only* page 107.
While you are flipping, be sure you
can see the picture on page 107
and the one on page 109.
If you flip quickly, the two
pictures will start to look like
<u>one</u> *animated* picture.

Don't forget to add
your own sound-effects!

LEFT HAND HERE

RICKY'S ROBOT
BATTLED HARDER.

RICKY'S ROBOT
BATTLED HARDER.

FLIP-O-RAMA 5

(pages 111 and 113)

Remember, flip *only* page 111.
While you are flipping, be sure you
can see the picture on page 111
and the one on page 113.
If you flip quickly, the two
pictures will start to look like
<u>one</u> *animated* picture.

Don't forget to add
your own sound-effects!

LEFT HAND HERE

AND JUSTICE PREVAILED.

111

RIGHT THUMB HERE

**AND JUSTICE
PREVAILED.**

CHAPTER FOURTEEN
JUSTICE PREVAILS

The evil Voodoo Vultures were no
match for Ricky Ricotta's Mighty Robot.
"Let's get out of here!" moaned the
Vultures.

"Hey, wait for *ME*!"
cried Victor Von Vulture.
But it was too late.
The Voodoo Vultures flew back to
Venus and were never heard from again.

The Mighty Robot picked up Ricky, and together they took Victor Von Vulture to the Squeakyville jail.

"Boo-hoo-hoo!" cried Victor.

"Maybe now you will learn some responsibility!" said Ricky.

Then Ricky Ricotta and his Mighty
Robot flew straight home . . .

. . . just in time for supper.

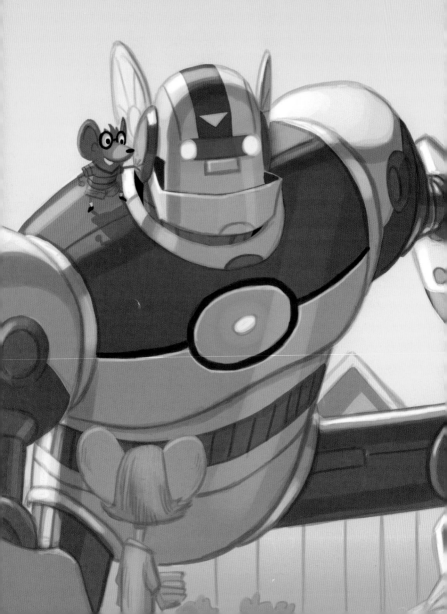

CHAPTER FIFTEEN
SUPPERTIME

Ricky's mother and father had cooked a wonderful feast for Ricky and his Mighty Robot.

"Oh, boy!" said Ricky. "TV dinners! My favorite!"

"We're both very proud of you boys," said Ricky's mother.

"Thank you for doing the right thing at the right time," said Ricky's father.

"No problem," said Ricky . . .

. . . "that's what friends are for!"

READY FOR

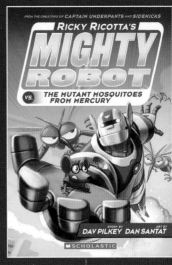

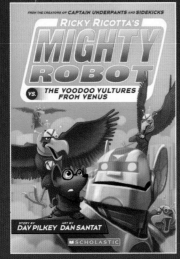

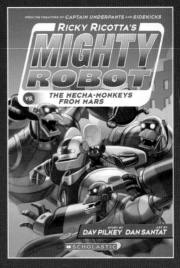

MORE RICKY?

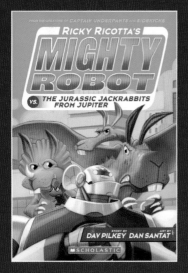

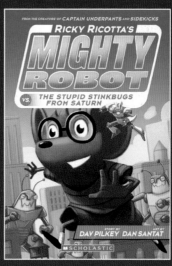

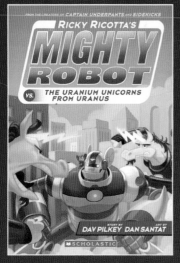

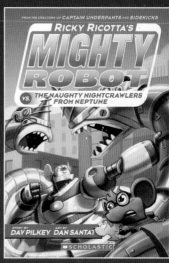

DAV PILKEY

has written and illustrated more than fifty books for children, including *The Paperboy*, a Caldecott Honor book; *Dog Breath: The Horrible Trouble with Hally Tosis*, winner of the California Young Reader Medal; and the IRA Children's Choice Dumb Bunnies series. He is also the creator of the *New York Times* best-selling Captain Underpants books. Dav lives in the Pacific Northwest with his wife. Find him online at www.pilkey.com.

DAN SANTAT

is the writer and illustrator of the picture book *The Adventures of Beekle: The Unimaginary Friend*. He is also the creator of the graphic novel *Sidekicks* and has illustrated many acclaimed picture books, including the *New York Times* bestseller *Because I'm Your Dad* by Ahmet Zappa and *Crankenstein* by Samantha Berger. Dan also created the Disney animated hit *The Replacements*. He lives in Southern California with his family. Find him online at www.dantat.com.